A Sweet Jam

HOUSHANG MORADI KERMANI

A Sweet Jam

Translated from the Persian
By Caroline Croskery

For Armita [...] ♡
With Best Wishes
Caroline Croskery
aug 2016

Printed by CreateSpace, An Amazon.com
Company
CreateSpace, Charleston, SC

First Edition, 2015.
Printed by CreateSpace

eStore address:
https://www.createspace.com/5303876

Available from Amazon.com and other retail outlets
Available on Kindle and other devices

ISBN-13: 978-1507886243
ISBN-10: 1507886241

Printed in the United States of America

Contents

Translator's Introduction

Houshang Moradi Kermani is a one-of-a-kind Iranian children's author, loved and revered internationally by people of all ages. His books have been translated into many languages because he has that special ability to tell universally familiar yet unpredictable stories. It is through his characters that he imparts human stories that reveal lessons many readers will have already learned the hard way. We always find something of ourselves, life, society, family and nostalgia in his works – but we're never quite sure how things will turn out in the end. While the stories are culturally Iranian, people of all ages and nationalities enjoy them.

This is my second opportunity to translate a work by Houshang Moradi Kermani into English and it is with the utmost pleasure that I share this sweet story with you.

How can such a small issue escalate all out of proportion? Small issues grow into big ones when a community is interconnected. This story will hook you right from page one. Read on!

Caroline Croskery

Chapter One

He stuck his tongue out the side of his mouth, grit his teeth, turned red, and then redder but with all the force he was exerting, it still wouldn't open.

"Darn, I'll get you open!"

He got down onto his knees on the kitchen floor and placed the jar between his legs, holding the jar tightly with his left hand, wrapping his right hand around the lid, and twisting the lid with all the strength he could muster in his arms – but to no avail. It wouldn't open. *What's wrong with this jar!*

"I can't get it open! It's so tight!"

"Then forget about it," said his mother, "you're going to be late. The school bell is going to ring any minute now!"

While still trying to get the lid off, Jalal said, "I bought the jam so that I could eat it, and I won't stop trying until I get it open!"

"What are you doing? Give it to me! Can't a big guy like you get a simple jar of jam open? All you know how to do is act tough! Just a dreamer! You act so mighty! Uh...this lid really won't come off."

Jalal laughed. Mother was talking and twisting as she tried to turn the lid but was not able to open the jar.

"Now, can't you just *not* eat jam for a day? You're so stubborn. Stubborn!"

Mother put the jar of jam under the scalding, hot faucet water. Her hands must have burned but she didn't show it. Work had left her hands calloused and used to extreme hot and cold. There was steam rising from the lid of the jar. She took a rag and wrapped it around the top of the jar and was trying to twist off the lid when Jalal grabbed it from her saying, "Now that the lid is warm, it will opcn easily."

"Yes, opening a jar requires know-how not strength! Muscles don't solve every problem!"

Jalal put the cloth around the top of the jar and twisted as hard as he could. His face became contorted as his mother watched.

"You still can't open it! Give it to me!"

This time mother ran the lid under the boiling water from the samovar. Jalal said, "Give it to me!"

"No! I'll open it myself. You go get your notebooks and books together and get dressed so you can leave as soon as you eat breakfast."

Mother was twisting hard trying to open the jar while she spoke. "No, it's no use! I can't do this. It won't open! See how you're wasting my time with this? I took a day off today to try and get some things done around here and go over to the insurance company."

No, it wasn't opening – not with the piece of cloth, nor without it. Jalal took the jar of jam, opened the apartment door and went downstairs to the neighbor's. Mr. Zeinali was getting dressed for work. Jalal handed him the jar of jam and asked, "Would you please open this for me?"

"You mean a big boy like you can't open a jar of jam himself? When I was your age I could climb straight up the walls! How old are you?"

"Twelve and a half."

Mr. Zeinali asked his wife for a dish towel and put it over the top of the lid, His face tightened as his tongue stuck out of the side of his mouth and then he grit his teeth and turned red as he twisted. "No, it's not possible. You got to put it under some hot water, and then it will open."

"We did that," Jalal remarked, "but it wouldn't open. The threads in the lid are probably stripped that it won't open."

"How could the threads be stripped? It's just like anything else. Turn it to the left and it opens, turn it to the right and it tightens." And then Mr. Zeinali yelled, "Madam, get me a knife please!"

Jalal said, "And there's not even anything written on the jar, like an arrow or instructions on how to get it open easily. We've wasted all this time!"

A car horn sounded from the next street. Mr. Zeinali left the jar and the knife, put on his coat and grabbed his shoes. "I'm sorry. My ride is here. Put the tip of the knife under the lid and try prying it open by hammering the butt of the knife a few times. It will open. It's probably vacuum shut. Maybe it's screwed on wrong, or if the jam is really old and expired it might have rusted. Who did you buy it from?"

"I bought it from Mr. Ahmad, the grocer at the corner store."

The honking sound came again. This time it was longer. Mr. Zeinali got on his shoes quickly, flew down the stairs and went out as his wife called after him, "Don't forget to buy some tuna from the store." Mr. Zeinali didn't hear it. He was running out to the street.

Jalal went back up to his apartment, grabbed a kitchen knife, edged it under the lid and then twisted. He heard his mother warn as she stripped the beds, "You're going to break that knife.

13

This is the only one left out of my set of six knives! You're going to break this one too!" Jalal was determined to get the jar open. He hammered the butt of the knife several times to loosen the lid, but to no avail. The lid just wouldn't open, even though the lid was now misshapen and crooked. It was jammed.

He hastily stuffed a large bite of bread and cheese into his mouth and with bulging cheeks he called, "I'm out of here, mom!"

He put the jar of jam into his backpack as he left, his mother calling behind him, "Where are you taking that jar of jam? What's wrong with you?"

"My classmates are really strong! They'll get it open."

"But the jar might break and you'll get cut! You're going to cause all kinds of problems and they'll call me down to the school again. I can't keep coming over there every single day! Don't take that jar of jam. I'm afraid you'll break it!"

"Don't worry, mom!" Jalal quickly leapt down the stairs with his mother calling behind him, "If I'm not home when you get back from school, the key will be at Mrs. Zeilali's house." Jalal was already out running down the street.

Chapter Two

The children gathered around Jalal in the classroom as his jar of jam was causing a stir. Standing on the bench and holding up the jar of jam for all to see, he yelled, "Hey you guys! Be quiet! Bahadori first!"

Bahadori was tall and strong. Puffing himself up, he smiled and came forward. The kids all stood back to let him through. "What will you give me if I open it in one try?"

"You can have the whole jar for yourself! Eat it and get fat!"

One of the kids said, "Bahadori is a nice guy. He'll share it with us!"

Bahadori smirked at the kid, "Get out of my way!"

He took the jar in his hands, with his long fingers positioned around the lid, and twisted it confidently. The jar wouldn't open. He tried again. The kids began to clap for him. He put his foot up onto the bench with the jar of jam on his knee, so that he had more control over the jar.

One of the kids hit him on the arm, "You're an embarrassment!"

Bahadori said, "Get lost!"

His face became contorted as he twisted even harder. But instead of twisting the lid on the jar, the twisting movement went through his body. The kids thought he succeeded in opening the jar, and yelled "Hoorah!" and clapped. "Long live Bahardori!"

He turned to them, "Be quiet! Shut up! Let me see what I'm doing here!"

"You mean you didn't open it?"
Jalal went forward to take back the jar of jam, but Bahadori wouldn't let him have it. "You coward, you glued the lid shut at home to play a trick on me, didn't you?"

"Get lost! Quit your whining! None of us were able to open it at our house! Give it to me!"

Afshari was a skinny, frail kid who would always sit under a tree in the school yard reading a book during PE. He took the jar of jam.

Bahadori rolled his eyes at Jalal which meant, "If you're up to something to make me look bad, I'll fix you! You're not going to get away with it." He wiped the sweat from his brow and stood innocently in the corner of the classroom.

Afshari subjected the jar and lid to his scientific scrutiny. "So you said no one has been able to open this? Ok, I'll open it."

The other kids taunted him saying, "Dare you! Dare you! Dare you!"

"Oh, you're taunting me, are you? What if I open it?"

Jalal said, "Then you can have it!"

"I don't like cherry jam."

"Then I'll give you a hundred tomans."

Afshari went and stood on the bench. He held up the jar and spun around to show all sides, just like a magician. Then he got down off the bench.

He took some chalk dust and rubbed it into the palms of his hands. Then he got back up on the bench. Everybody was watching him in silence. Afshari took the jar again, showed it to the children and turned to Jalal. "One hundred tomans? You've got a deal."

"Deal!" Jalal replied.

He held the jar in his right hand, took a deep breath and began twisting the lid of the jar with his left hand. He was left-handed. Turning the lid ever so gently and patiently, convincingly acting as if he had succeeded in opening the jar, Afshari smiled victoriously. They all thought he had opened it. "Clap for me!"

"Kids get back to your seats! Afshari! Get down off that bench! Where are your manners?" It was Mr. Hassani, the history teacher. "You all get back to your seats! If the teacher is a few minutes late, that doesn't give you the right to horse around and make a lot of noise! Whose jar is that?"

"Sir, it's Jalal Pourzand's. He wasn't able to get the lid open at home and so he brought it to school to have us open it. Can you do it?" Afshari gave the jar to the teacher.

Inspecting the jar, he said, "It's obvious you've really worked on it. You've even beat the lid. And it still wouldn't open? A person should use his brains first, and then his muscles. You ought to figure out why it won't open. That's the secret. The world's scientists always look for the 'whys' of things. Why won't this open? Not being able to get the lid open could be due to many reasons."

The teacher began writing on the board.

"The expiration of shelf life and decomposition of the contents of the jar may have produced gasses which caused a vacuum state to occur inside the jar, preventing it from being opened.

"The lid is a few millimeters smaller than the neck of the jar. At the factory, the jar was sealed tightly by a machine and will now not open.

"During the filling of the jar, the jam was extremely hot, which caused the glass jar to expand. The jar was closed easily, but now that the jar has cooled down, the metal lid has contracted and will not open. The jam should have been cooled before having been poured into the jar."

Jalal said, "What should we do now, sir? As the scholar, you should help us find the answer to this question so we won't be distracted by this problem all day."

"The jar should be put under hot water."

"Excuse me, sir. My mother put the jar under hot water and it still wouldn't open. Sir, can you open it?"

"No. Seeing that you haven't been able to open it, I won't be able to either. If I succeed, all the students will say that it was not a big deal because the teacher was big and strong. And if I don't succeed, they will all laugh and say that the teacher, who thought of himself as a scientist and scholar, wasn't able to open it! So it's better if I refrain from trying. In any case, for me it would end in failure. Throughout history, I know there have been a lot of fails and I don't knows. I am not a PE or a science teacher. Ask me what happened during the Qajar Dynasty, and I'll lecture you for a whole month. But I can't open a simple jar of jam. At least I don't deem it advisable to do so. Pourzand, put the jar of jam into your backpack and don't cause any further distraction of the class. It would be better if you asked questions about your lesson."

The kids passed the jar back to him and each tried to open it as it went.

"Pourzand! Take your jar of jam to the office. When you're ready to go home, you can take it with you. And don't bring these kinds of things to school again. Opening or not opening a jar of jam has nothing to do with history. History deals with the past. Opening a jar of jam is a present issue."

Jalal got the jar of jam back and walked it down to the office. The principal said, "What's this?"

"It's a jar of jam. I can't get it open. Mr. History teacher said to bring it to the office."

"Why did you bring this to school?"

"I wanted to see if the kids could help me get it open. But nobody was able to."

"So you've caused a ruckus for nothing. Put it over there near that potted plant and go back to class."

When Jalal was gone, the principal took his turn trying to open the jar.

At recess, Jalal looked through the glass window in the office door and saw the teachers around the jar of jam trying to get it open, but they couldn't. It wouldn't open. The science teacher was holding it as he stood in the middle of the office, explaining from the standpoint of physics and chemistry, why it wouldn't open. The teachers tried one by one to open it. But it wouldn't open. It just wouldn't open.

Chapter Three

Jalal and five or six of the kids poured into the corner grocer's. "What's going on? What do you kids want?"

Jalal turned and ordered the kids, "Wait outside."

They went out to the sidewalk reluctantly and peered back into the shop through the glass to see how the grocer was going to open the jar of jam. The grocer was busy with two other customers. Jalal waited for them to do their shopping and leave before he said, "Mr. Ahmad, if it is possible, could you please open this jar of jam for me?"

"What's wrong with it? The jam is fresh. They just delivered it to me. Is it sour? Has it molded?"

"No. Open it."

However hard the grocer tried, he wasn't able to get it open. He took some cloth and wrapped it around the lid, but still was not able to open it. He inspected the lid. "You should have run it under hot water."

The other kids were now back inside the shop, watching the grocer. "What do you folks want? What are you doing in here?"

"They've all come inside to see how you are going to get this thing open."

"It won't open."

"Then give me another one," said Jalal.

"You've already banged on it and scratched the lid, and now the threads are stripped. The factory won't take it back." The grocer thought a little, and took another one just like it from the shelf and played with it. No matter what he did, he couldn't get it open. The kids laughed and annoyed him, "Heh, heh, heh...you think that's funny? Get on out of here! Little brats!"

Jalal said, "Well, open another one. Let's at least see how the rest of the jams are."

The grocer took another jar. No matter what he did, no matter how hard he tried, he put it under hot water, he banged on the lid, but he couldn't get it open. It wouldn't open at all.

All the kids were laughing.

The grocer grabbed a piece of hose to chase the kids out of his shop. He ran around from behind the refrigerator towards them. They all backed out of the shop to the sidewalk.

The grocer turned to Jalal, "Well, the other jars won't open either. I don't know. I don't know what is wrong with them."

"Well, then just take this one and give me my money back."

"You have destroyed the lid. The factory won't take it back."

A woman came inside the shop to buy some yogurt. The grocer took a pail of yogurt out of the refrigerator.

Jalal said, "Well what should I do now?"

"For heaven's sake, I've been a grocer for twenty years and I never seen anything like this happen before. None of them will open!"

The woman was listening and said, "A few days ago I bought a jar of whey. No matter what we did, we couldn't get the jar open. I still have it. I'm pretty sure it's no longer any good."

Jalal said, "Well what should I do? Give me my money back."

The woman said, "A person should file a complaint against these new factories opening every day that are sending defective merchandise into the market and close them down or make them pay damages to their customers!"

One of the kids called Jalal, pulled him aside, and whispered something in his ear. Jalal took back his jar of jam that was sitting on top of the case and left the shop.

Jalal walked down the sidewalk with jar in hand, the kids all following after him. "Jalal, did he pay your money back? Will you treat us?"

"You don't have to do much, just buy us each an ice cream cone. Buy us those expensive ones!"

Chapter Four

After the kids all left, the grocer began to think to himself *what is the meaning of this! How could it be possible for none of these lids to open?* He twisted hard on the lid of each jar, but none of them would open. When the customers would come into the shop, they would notice that he was preoccupied, perplexed and irritable.

He was up on the stool taking the jars of jam off of the shelves, trying to get the jars open, but he grumbled and cursed as he couldn't. Whatever the customers asked of him, he would simply reply, "I don't have it ma'am! I don't have it, sir. We're all out boy. I don't have any, young lady. Go buy it elsewhere. Leave me alone."

The floor of the shop was covered with jars of jam. It angered the grocer to see them all. His usual customers, the neighbors, felt sorry for him. They said, "You're getting old, Mr. Ahmad. What's wrong? Can't you get the lids open?"

A big truck stopped in front of the shop. The food distributor got out of the truck with a form and pen in hand. "Hello, how are you? What would you like today? We have carrot, fig, berry or citron jam."

The grocer was sitting on the floor in the middle of his shop holding his knees, deep in thought. He was staring at the jars of jam. "Are you listening to me, Mr. Ahmad? What are you thinking about? Snap out of it! I say hello to you and you don't even answer me!"

The man walked behind the counter, put his hand on the grocer's shoulder and said loudly, "Hello!"

The grocer gave a start and jumped to attention. He blinked his eyes a few times and looked around. "Something happened today that has completely puzzled me. I think I must be dreaming. Pray that I'm only dreaming, otherwise I'll break every single one of these jars of jam myself! Just tell me I'm dreaming and put my mind at ease. In twenty years as a grocer, I have never seen anything like this before. Open this! Take it! Take it! All of the jars! Take them all! Open it, sir! Open it!"

"Why do you want me to open it? What are you talking about?" The grocer thrust a jar of jam into his hand. "Go ahead. Open this one!"

With a distrusting smirk on his face, the distributor took the jar, and however hard he twisted, the jar wouldn't open.

"Well, maybe it's just this one jar."

"No, sir! No, my dear sir. None of these will open. I've lost my reputation in the neighborhood over this, sir."

"You've lost your reputation in the neighborhood over a jar of jam not opening? What do you mean?"

"Yes, sir, ever since this morning, no, since noon I've been trying to figure out how is it that none of them can be opened. A young boy came into my shop with a complaint and he is going to file suit against your factory.

"A woman came into the store and was angry saying, 'You should be ashamed of yourself, Mr. Ahmad! Now you refuse to sell to my daughter? She came in here to buy some cake! And you told her to go somewhere else? And by the way, that jar of whey you sold me won't open! Did I ask for it for free? You have all these jars of whey! So sell them!'

"She had come into the shop for some whey. So I told her, 'I can't sell them, ma'am, until I figure out where I stand with this factory. I'm not going to sell another thing until that time. I won't sell anything that comes in a jar. Not jam, not honey, not tomato paste, and not whey! And I'm not selling hogwash, rubbish or poppycock either! I'm not selling anything! I have a reputation to uphold! The other day I sold two jars of whey and the lids won't open! I tried so hard to get them open, but I couldn't. I can't fight with people all day long over it! And now today these lids won't open!' The woman grumbled, dropped her head and left."

The grocer looked the distributor straight in the eyes, "Now you see, sir?

That's how my reputation has become sullied in this neighborhood!"

"What do you mean by that?"

"I mean you keep asking 'what do you mean?' What do you mean? Instead of that, try opening one of your jars! Try distributing decent merchandise to people. They don't buy the jam to sweeten their mouths by licking the outside of the jar! They want to actually eat the jam! They want to butter their bread and spread jam on top of it and put that bite into their mouths and eat it! That's it! They can't rub the bread on the outside of the jar and say 'yummy'!"

The truck driver kept honking, but the grocer and the distributor who were in the middle of their argument paid no attention. Finally, the truck driver got down out of the truck and came into the store. "Mr. Jafari, why are you taking so long? The police will come and ticket me, man!"

The grocer said, "Driver, come over here and open one of these jars. You are young and have strong arms." The driver took the jar of jam, but no matter how hard he twisted, it still wouldn't open. He tried another one. No matter what he did, he couldn't get one open. "This is strange." The grocer said, "That's exactly what I've been saying. But nobody believes that it's strange. And this man here keeps saying 'what do you mean? What do you mean?' Ask yourself this question. Ask your factory! You ought to be ashamed of this merchandise. You've made me crazy! I'm going to file a complaint!"

The driver said, "I'm the driver. I have a first class commercial driver's license. That's all I do. I don't open jars of jam. It's not my job. Ask me where the gear box is; ask me how far it is from here to the factory – that's the kind of stuff I know."

A police officer rolled up on his motorcycle, "This truck should be moved. Truck driver, move your truck." The truck driver walked out of the store. The officer asked him, "Why did you leave this truck here unattended?"

"Sir, officer, a strange thing has happened. They can't get the lids off on some jars of jam. Not even one!"

The officer got off of his motorcycle. The grocer handed him a jar of jam. "Go ahead, open it!" The officer passed him his ticketing pad to hold. But no matter how hard he tried, he couldn't get the jar open. "I'm a police officer. This issue has nothing to do with me. These jars not opening is not the responsibility of the police. This truck has to move. He wrote out the ticket, handed it to the driver, got onto his motorcycle and left.

The butcher next door heard the noise and commotion coming from Ahmad's shop, so he came to see what was going on. He also tried his hand at one of the jars, as did several passersby. Each one of them picked up a jar and twisted hard. The shop and the sidewalk outside were growing crowded with people. The neighborhood patrol stopped by, "What's going on over here. Why are so many people gathering outside of this shop?"

"Captain, sir, we can't get these jars open. Please, go ahead and try one yourself." The officer took one, positioned himself securely and twisted. Passersby would stand gawking curiously at the police patrol vehicle and the crowds outside the shop. Some of them would venture forward, take a jar and try their hand at twisting. But nobody succeeded in opening one.

The police announced on the loudspeaker, "Ladies and gentlemen, disperse! A jar of jam not opening is not a spectator sport! Disperse!"

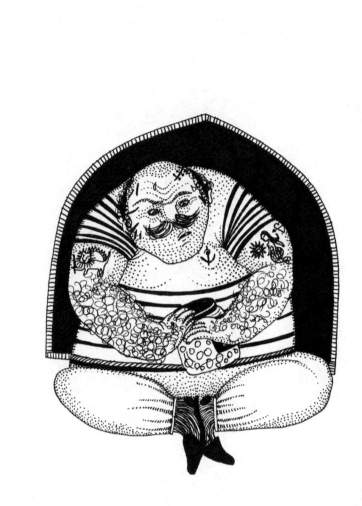

Chapter Five

With jar of jam in hand, Jalal walked ahead with a gaggle of kids following after him. When they reached the police station, they saw a security officer standing watch in the guard house at the entrance to the station.

"We have a complaint, sir," as they walked right past him.

"Hey! Where do you think you're going?" said the guard.

"I told you, we have a complaint."

The guard laughed. "That's not how we do things. Children are not permitted inside the police station."

"We're not children. We're grown up and we have a complaint. Your boss is our neighbor, and we want to see him. We have a question to ask him."

"Okay, now that you're grown up, you can go in. But just one of you!" Jalal shot a knowing glance at the others and handed his backpack for his classmate, Ghaffouri to hold. With his jar of jam in hand, he went inside.

He walked through the hubbub inside the station, passing by multifarious characters, delinquents, street fighters and criminals on his way to see an officer.

"What do you want, son?"

Jalal, who had never seen a place like that before, felt timid. He put the jar on the table and said, "Excuse me, sir. I can't get this lid open."

The officer picked up the jar of jam, inspected it carefully and asked, "Is it contaminated? Has it spoiled? Was it overpriced?" He tried to open the lid, but however hard he tried, he couldn't.

He asked, "Where are your parents? If you have a complaint, you'll have to come back with them...What is the meaning of this? Why won't this open?"

"That's why I'm complaining, sir. I can't get the lid open. Why should they sell jam if the lids won't open? It doesn't make any difference whether you're a child or an adult!"

"Hold it under some hot water. Go on! Don't waste my time over these trivial matters!"

"I did hold it under hot water, but it still wouldn't open. And as for trivial matters, big issues begin with little ones. That's what my literature teacher, Mr. Mozaffari always says."

The officer grumbled, "I've never seen a complaint like this one before! A jar of jam won't open and they want to file a complaint over it!" With a smirk on his face, he read what was written on the lid, "Finest quality. Sour Cherry Jam. Shabdar Factory. Contents: Cherries, Sugar...Manufacture file no. M6526473 of the Ministry of Food Safety, 5555. Keep in a cool place. Gross weight: 300 grams. Retail price..........Rials. Yes, they've left the price blank. That's not our problem. If you have an issue with the price, you'll have to report it to the Bureau of Business

Affairs. If it's spoiled, you have to go to the Ministry of Food Safety. They'll tell you what to do there. Now go on. You can find the address and phone number right on the jar of jam. You can go there. Now go on!"

"Where is the Ministry of Food Safety?"

"It's right down the street. Ask as you go so you won't get lost. Go tomorrow morning."

As Jalal walked out of the guard's room, he saw himself surrounded by street fighters and muggers lining the hallways of the police station. They grabbed his jar of jam and were wrestling each other for their turn to twist it open – but it wouldn't open.

A tall hooligan type with a big belly, cursed and sweat and twisted as hard as he could – but it wouldn't open. He wanted to angrily throw the jar against the wall. Jalal grabbed his wrist, "Don't break it! Give it to me!"

"You really oughta sue that factory! They call that a jar of jam?"

They passed the jar around, but none of them could get it open. The guard took the jar from the ruffians and handed it back to Jalal as he sent him out of the station. "Go on out of here. Go on little boy. Go demand your rights."

48

Chapter Six

It was chaos on the sidewalk in front of the grocer. People were climbing over one another to get a glimpse of what was going on. The street was jammed with cars; drivers were sticking their heads out of their windows:

"What's going on? What's happening?"

"I don't know but whatever it is, it's going on over there inside the grocer's."

"They say they found a snake in there."

"The store owner had a heart attack."

"They've caught a shoplifter. They're holding the thief there until the police arrive."

"No sir, I went over there and saw that their jars of jam won't open. People are gathering to see why they won't open."
Ahmad the grocer took all the jars down off his shelf, boxed them up and handed them back to the distributor, "You have to take these back. You've ruined my reputation with this substandard merchandise of yours!"

The distributor had no choice. He picked up the boxes, walked right past the grocer's customers and loaded the boxes of defective jars of jam onto the truck.
The police patrol car blasted from its loudspeaker, "Food distributor truck move forward!" The police were disbursing the people.

"What is going on, sir?"

"Go on! Go on! Nothing has happened."

People were talking with each other as they left the grocer's shop.

"All the jars of jam were contaminated."

"It was some kind of contamination that happened at the factory. There were bacteria in the jam. They are recalling them. Several people died already from eating the jams."

"No, that's not true at all!"

"Then what's the story?"

"The jars won't open. I saw it myself."

"That's just what they are saying. And you bought it? They're planning on hiking up the price. First they collect the entire inventory and then they jack up the price."

"Well, let's go buy some before they do that!"

Chapter Seven

The truck driver pulled over, got out and went into a telephone booth.

"Hello? Mr. Sabahi? Something strange happened today. The jars of jam won't open. It started with one grocer. I think his customers complained...yes, whatever we did the jars wouldn't open. And the jars from today's delivery won't open either. The driver and I weren't able to get any of them open. Yes...yes...and we went to two other grocers to check out the prior deliveries and those won't open either. What do you want me to do? What should I do?"

The distributor was going into the stores saying, "Hello, I'm here to take back any jars of jam you may have from our factory."

"Why? Why are you recalling the jams?"

"There's a problem with them."

The grocers all wondered what was going on. The telephones started ringing, "Hassan sir, salaam, how are you? Are they recalling the products coming from the Shabdar factory?"

"Asghar, they're recalling the jam from the Shabdar factory. Be on your guard."

The telephone would ring, and then the delivery boys would immediately hop onto their motor scooters, bicycles and even run down the sidewalks.

"They're recalling all the jam from the Shabdar factory!"

It was bedlam inside the shops. They were taking down all the jam from the shelves and some of them were hiding it.

"No, we don't have any, sir."

"No, we're all out, madam."

"We have some, but I'm not sure if it's ok. You'll buy it and then return it in two days and ask me what kind of merchandise that was I sold you!"

"Well, just give me a few jars anyway. I'm your customer. We heard it was all a trick. They're planning on raising the price."

"What kind of jam do you want?"

"Any kind you have left; the more, the better!"

The news was spreading to the customers and community. Everybody wanted jam. On the other hand, the distributor trucks were going around recalling it all. The other factory owners heard that Shabdar was recalling all its jams and so they notified their distributors, "You are recalling all your jam, honey and whey. If you raise the price, we will do the same, and why shouldn't we? Raw materials and labor have gone up, yet the price of the goods has stayed low and hasn't moved."

56

Chapter Eight

Lining both sides of the hallway were glass cases which held all sorts of items: toys, molding clay, pesticide, plant food, shampoo, tomato paste, cola, shortening, dry milk, face cream, powder, disposable cups, cookies, all kinds of jams and so on.

Jalal was scrutinizing every item in the case as he walked down the hallway. He was still holding the jar of jam. As he looked at all those items, he wondered what kind of ministry this could be.

A man in a white smock passed him.

"Hello, sir."

"Yes, how can I help you?"

Jalal held out the jar of jam. "I brought this here to find out why the lid won't open."

The man pointed towards the door to an office, and kept walking.

Jalal read the plaque outside the office door. "Containers and Packaging." He timidly went inside. A slender woman wearing glasses sat at a desk. She was looking at something very small under a microscope. She was inundated with cans and boxes.

Quivering, Jalal asked, "Excuse me, ma'am. This jar of jam won't open."At first she thought it was just a little brat coming in there to play a trick on her. But when she perceived his fear, she realized that a kid playing tricks wouldn't be afraid and wouldn't shake like that. Besides, he was holding an actual jar. She got up and took it from him. She inspected it carefully and saw that it wouldn't open.

She called for help from the woman in the next office but the woman wasn't successful in getting it opened either. She hit hard on the lid several times with a knife handle, but to no avail. She was about to put it under hot water when Jalal said, "We've put it under hot water already. And we hit the lid several times too. We wedged the tip of a knife under the lid but it wouldn't open. So they told us to bring it to the Ministry of Food Safety, here to you."

The second woman was heavyset. She snarled and said under her breath, "What could it be!"

Jalal said, "Yes, what could it be? Every person who has seen it asks this same question. Now is it possible to file a complaint against the factory?"

"Yes, as the consumer, you have the right to file a complaint."

"That the lid won't open?"

"Yes, you can file a complaint about the defective packaging of the food product. That it is too hard to open. We have had cases where the consumer was using a knife to open a jar and the tip of the knife broke off and lodged in the eye, or another case when the consumer was trying very hard to twist off the lid which caused the jar to break and injure the person's hand. Since the lid was old and rusted, the person got tetanus and died. And so the factory now has to pay damages for that consumer."

"What do they give to the consumer?"

"You will receive damages – money."

He felt excited. Jalal's eyes sparkled. He puckered up his lips, his mouth watering in delight. And he was no longer afraid.

"How much will they pay me?"

"That depends on your losses."

"What should I do next?"

"You'll take this jar to the Food and Hygiene Products Inspection Office, and leave it there along with a statement of fact, and you'll demand your rights. Of course, your elders will have to accompany you."

"If they don't give me any answer, then what?"

"If they don't answer? You see, if the jam is contaminated or the basic ingredients are defective somehow, they will find out by taking a sample and performing chemical and pathological tests on it, then the factory owner would be convicted and they would order the factory closed forever or for a designated time and the factory would lose a lot of money. And that is why they would rather seek your satisfaction in the case."

"You mean they would pay any amount of money to get my satisfaction?"

"That's right! You're a smart little boy!"

"But what if all that stuff you said wasn't the case, and it was just that the lid wouldn't open, then what? Would I still have any rights? Would they still pay me damages?"

"Yes, yes, why do you ask so many questions?"

"Excuse me, one more question. It's very important. What should I write in the letter?"

"Write, 'I, the consumer, do hereby state that the lid of this jar of jam is defective, and the tip of the knife will break off and fly into my eye."

And the women laughed. The woman who was looking into the microscope handed Jalal a form and said, "Write:

Head Office for the Inspection
of Food and Hygienic Products
Dear Sirs,

The Shabdar Factory has not observed hygienic conditions in the production of jam. At the present time, I, the consumer suspect the probability of contamination in and illness from this product. Under these circumstances, I request preliminary inspection of the production facility."

"But I haven't written anything about the lid not opening."

"Write 'Lastly, I would like to inform you that the lid of the product will not open.'"

"Excuse me, ma'am. My teacher said it is incorrect to say the lid will not open. We should say that the lid cannot 'be opened'".

"Ok fine. You say it that way."

"Let's write that it cannot be opened 'at all'".

"Ok, fine. Write 'it cannot be opened at all'. Now you have to rewrite the letter in nice handwriting and come back with your mom and dad and bring this jar of jam and submit them to the office I mentioned."

"Oh, I'm going to be late. I've got to get to class. I'll do it tomorrow."

Jalal was happy as he ran to school with the jar of jam and the letter in hand.

Chapter Nine

Mother was sitting at a table working. She was making chalk markings on the front of girls' overcoats where the buttons would be sewn on by someone else.

Mother worked at a textile factory. Her hands worked quickly and efficiently, but her mind was not on her work.

What disaster has he brought upon himself this time? Has he been hit by a car? Has he hit his head on the curb and fallen unconscious in the gutter, the driver sped off and people taken him to the hospital? *Maybe they've looked in his backpack and found his school ID and found the school's telephone number on it. Did you even take your card? You keep losing it! I keep finding it and putting it in your bag, and you take it out and leave it everywhere! Have you written your name on your notebooks? I hope you didn't go with the other kids to the park or to the cinema! No, you're not that disobedient. You'll be in big trouble if you played hooky from school and went to the movies! You wouldn't dare do something like that without my permission! You're in trouble Jalal. You have no brains. Did he take that jar of jam or not? I can't remember. Did you put that jar in your pocket trying to hide it from me? It wouldn't fit in there. You put it in your bag. Didn't you think it might break? Or the lid would open up and get jam all over your notebooks and books? Oh, what am I saying? That jar won't even open! You're so bad, Jalal! Watch what happens when I get my hands on you! You think you're all grown up? You've got a lot of growing up to do! I'll teach you a lesson or two! Who do you think you are! Your poor late father, what fault is it of his? It's my fault the way I spoiled you. Remember that day when you went up to the corner to buy a newspaper? When did you come back? Three hours later! I was so worried about you! Then when you got back you said the first shop didn't have one, so you went to the next shop, and they didn't have one, so you went to the next shop after that and on and on until the end of the street, to the other end of town. Well, what the hell if they didn't have a newspaper! You should have come right home! To hell with it if the lid of the jar of jam won't open! Throw it away! Will you die if you don't eat jam for one day? I'll take that jar and hit you over the head with it, I will! Look what you've done to my nerves? Look how I'm shaking! Look at my hands! Look at them shaking! Look how pale I am! Where am I supposed to find you?*

"What's wrong? Why are you crying, Mrs. Pourzand?"

"Jalal, Jalal didn't go to school today. He wasn't present at first hour. The assistant supervisor called here. I told them to call here whenever there was a problem."

"Well, get up and go after him."

"Where should I look? He took that jar of jam that wouldn't open and I don't know where he's gone with it."

Mother cried and talked while she chalked the girls' overcoats.

Chapter Ten

Jalal was running through the streets. He had the jar of jam in hand and the letter tucked inside one of his books as he ran into the school yard.

"Where have you been, Mr. Pourzand?" The assistant supervisor saw him from the second floor window. "Come upstairs."

Jalal forced the jar of jam into his pocket and went up.

"Where were you?"

"Sir, we had literature first hour. I thought our teacher wasn't going to be here. He's been sick. I've been on errands."

"Where? What kind of errands? What is this?" And he touched the jar protruding from his pocket.

"Oh, that's jam. The lid won't open, so I've gone to file a complaint."

The assistant supervisor looked amused. "You've filed a complaint over not being able to open a jar of jam? And you expect me to believe that?! Now get to class! Slacker!"

Chapter Eleven

The general manager of the factory held the jar of jam in his hand as he stood there talking.

"This is strange. So strange. Unbelievable! I can't believe we have been producing and delivering a defective product to the market for two months, yet no one has said a word about it. No one has wondered why these lids won't open. No one has brought the factory or its packaging procedures under question. When the unknowing consumers realized the lid could not be opened, the first thing they thought to do was to put it under hot faucet water or the boiling water of a samovar and then twist as hard as possible. When they saw that it was no use, they abandoned their efforts. But the more determined and penny-pinching kind who agonized over their loss, took knifes or anything sharp they could get their hands on and started working on the lid, and of course cut themselves in the process. Or the tip of the knife broke off, flew into their eye and blinded them. What sweet and wonderful citizens we have! But, but unfortunately not even, not even one person ever thought the problem was the defective packaging on our part. Not only is the factory's packaging director responsible for this imprecision, but we are all responsible, from me, the general manager of this factory, all the way down to Mr. Esmaili, the gate guard. This is not a joke. If the authorities find out about this, they'll close us down right then and there! And all of the laborers, engineers and office workers will be out of a job. All of our investment will be lost. And more important than anything is that the monies spent on advertising our products will be lost. The people will lose their trust in Shabdar's sweet jams.

"Right now, right now as I'm speaking with you from the factory, in homes, on the shelves in kitchens, on top of refrigerators, next to stoves and dishwashers, behind chairs, and even in children's closets are thousands of jars of jam that no one has been able to open, and still no one has the diligence to pursue the problem. It's not for me, the general manager to deal with these kinds of issues. But it is something that has happened. We have recalled most of the defective jars of jam in question. But what about the product still in homes? Do you realize how damaging it could be if people realized they could file a complaint about this issue at the Ministry of Food Safety? You cannot always count on people being meek and kind about these things."

"Sir, have you heard about the young boy who took his jar of jam over to the Ministry of Food Safety to file a complaint?"

"Yeah, I've heard some things. If that nosy kid hadn't stuck to the lid problem like a duck on a june bug, we might have sent our product out to the market for years and years to come. The jam would have found its way onto store shelves and kitchen cabinets and collected dust and no one would have said a word. It's true that what this little kid has done is bitter for us and we'd rather have his head. I hope he falls on his face and breaks his jar of jam! But he has served us with a warning.

"Now there are a few things we have to do. First we have to find out why the jars won't open. We have to find out the facts and solve the problem. Then we have to work together to recall all the jam from the stores and homes all the way down to the last jar. More important than anything is to get the kid's release on the lawsuit no matter what it takes, and get that jar of jam from him. I don't know how, but that jar of jam has to be taken away from him. With a reward, begging, or by force, I don't know how! But we have to do it with precision – systematically and thoughtfully so that we can produce quality jam and pour it into beautiful jars with streamline lids and send out the new product to the market and be trusted again by our dear customers. Let's not allow our competitors, peers and sworn enemies –

other factories – to take advantage of this small issue and send out the word to the newspapers and in effect...Mr. Esmaeili! Sir! I am speaking! And you keep twisting and turning and trying to open that jar of jam? What a shame! My whole concern is for you dear laborers – for us not to have to shut our doors and put you all out of work and ashamed in front of your wives and children! If the factory loses its reputation and goes up in smoke, all of us will lose our reputations as well. The smoke will only blow into our own eyes. This Mr. Esmaeili beats down my door for a loan because he wants to fund his daughter's wedding. And I don't even want to mention that other one – you all know who I am talking about. That one who shows up late to work every morning and leaves early too. He's standing over there in the corner with the plaid shirt and brown jacket on. The one with the thick mustache. He's a poet and has a good voice and sings well and plays the sitar. He lives right next door to the factory and is talking with the person sitting next to him right now. But I won't mention his name as I would never want to make anyone lose their reputation. Yes, this person who is staring me down with his beady eyes and chewing on his moustache sneaks over to my office three times a day, cocks his head to one side like a sad sack and whines about his misery, illness, being a renter and having no money. All he talks about is getting a loan or allowances for dependents or overtime or a raise. But out of fear of his wife, he has to sneak a cigarette in the bathroom. I know all about him. These are the things that only I know and would never tell anyone. I don't want to air anybody's dirty laundry and make them lose their reputation. That's not the kind of person I am.

"Anyway, dear fellow whose name I will not mention here among all his co-workers, know and be aware that if this factory gets closed down or a heavy fine is levied on it, it is all of us who will feel the pain."

"Sir, if things get better and people forget about the problem of the lids not opening, will the factory still raise the price of jam to compensate for loss? I have heard the other factories are all going to raise their prices on jam."

"That problem has to be addressed. Now that you all understand the factory's position, go find out why the lids won't open, and solve the other problems too. Sometimes I wish I had never been born to witness this day!"

Chapter Twelve

There was no jam to be found in the marketplace. There was absolutely no jam in the shops or the stores. The word had spread that, "They are recalling all the jams. They plan on hiking up the prices."

Whoever got there first, bought several jars of jam and took them home. The shops and store managers cleared the shelves when they saw people were grabbing up all the jam.

The factories were also recalling their jams. Stores were putting up signs in their windows that read: "We buy only Shabdar jams."

The jam from the Shabdar factory was the most expensive of all. They would say that there was gold mixed in the metal of the lids. If a person melted the lid, they could get gold from it. Some people even collected the empty jars. The ones that had a ring in the glass at the bottom of the jar were considered to be worth more. They kept saying these jars would be worth a lot more someday.

So many people were buying up all the jam. Jam was everywhere in people's homes, arranged jar by jar on top of their refrigerators, on their mantles, shelves, and in the kitchens on their countertops by the drain boards. Every kind of jam was selling out: carrot, sour cherry, fig, squash, barberry, strawberry, citron, rose petal, apple, apricot, and orange marmalade.

The co-op stores for laborers and office workers were issuing coupon booklets for jam. When the employees would get off the buses and minivans coming home from work, you could see them carrying plastic shopping bags full of jams. On the streets and in stairwells of their buildings, friends and even strangers would stop and ask them, "Where are they selling jam? How much did you pay for it?"

After that, the employees and laborers would then wrap the jam in newspaper or carry it home in black plastic shopping bags so people wouldn't be able to tell what was in the bags and ply them with questions or jinx them with the evil eye.

There was jam everywhere: in the large front windows of the city busses, next to the drivers' packs of cigarettes and tea glasses and artificial flowers, or in the dashboard of taxis, or by the earthen pots next to clocks on the shelves of bread bakers' shops.

Co-ops and shops wouldn't sell the jam to their members and customers straight out either, but would only sell the jam with the purchase of another item. First they were selling the jam in tandem with bug spray. Then when the bug spray ran out, they sold it in tandem with adhesive bandages and then cotton swabs, the small kind mostly used for infants.

The laborers and office workers would protest, "Bug spray in the fall? Adhesive bandage without the need? Infant cotton swabs? What do we need all these for? Our homes are full of bug spray, adhesive bandage and cotton swabs! Why don't they quit this tyrannical inequity?"

After that, the co-ops stopped their tandem sales of bug spray, bandages and swabs, but started doing the same thing with shampoo, rugs and drinking glasses.

Outside every city, village and district shop, people would watch and sneer at the long lines of the jam-loving folk.

Chapter Thirteen

Jalal's mother insisted, "Even if you have a tantrum, I won't be coming over there with you to file a complaint. What do you think? What a ridiculous thing for an adult woman to go down there and file a formal complaint as to why a jar of jam won't open? To hell with the jar! If people just dropped all their responsibilities and went all over town filing complaints every time something went wrong then what would this world come to?.....like yesterday, when I was buying fruit at the green grocer's, as soon as I turned my head, that coward put three spoiled oranges into my bag and sold them to me with the four good ones. What about the dishwashing liquid I bought? I don't know what they put in that stuff but it is ruining my hands. This morning you bought fresh bread, but half of it was burnt and half was still like dough. You yourself, the last time you bought shoes, you were only able to wear them twice before they fell apart. I bought a box of dates. The first row on top was all nice and good quality dates. But underneath, they were all spoiled. If we had to complain over every little event, then we'd have to give up everything we normally do and go into the business of filing complaints full-time at this justice department and that courtroom, and make everyone in the universe dislike us."

Jalal said, "But this is different, mother."

"What do you mean, this is different? Anybody would double over laughing out loud to hear that you're filing a formal complaint over a jar of jam not opening. They would say you're either crazy or have nothing better to do. Or that you're naïve. Now look at you, you've caught a cold and are sniffling. Go peel yourself a couple of oranges. You've been spending too much time on this jar of jam. Don't waste your energy on this. You won't get anything out of it in the end."

"Look, let's go show our complaint to Mr. Zeinali. He'll know whether our complaint will get us any good results or not."

"No, it won't, I assure you. People will just laugh at us."

"Mother, what do you want me to buy for you when I get rich? A house with a lot of trees? And you won't have to work."

"Oh, that's just a pipe dream!"

"I'll get a good settlement. You'll see." Jalal peeked out of the window and saw that Mr. Zeinali's living room light was still on, but he was apparently in the middle of an argument with his wife. Their silhouettes looked like claws and teeth through the curtains. "Mom, they're having an argument."

"Oh, every time they have company, they argue after the guests leave over how the guests were, why he said something, or why she brought out the tea so late. They smile and laugh in front of the guests, but then after they leave..."

"No, mother, it's not about the guests. Come and listen!" You could hear Mr. Zeinali's voice and see his silhouette behind the curtain, shouting and waving his arms. "No ma'am, I am not a deadbeat! I buy the things we truly need for this household whenever they are needed. But we don't need jam! When have I ever bought jam before that suddenly I need to buy it now? Let the whole world go buy as much jam as it wants to! I for one and not buying any! I'm not a superficial person who only thinks about his stomach! And there are lots of people like me!"

"Why don't you learn from your colleagues? They buy and bring home milk, chicken and everything for their wife and children? That good friend of yours, Rezakhani – his wife told me that ever since he heard that there is a shortage of jam, he buys and brings home five or six jars a day! All kinds from squash jam to barberry jam! Don't you have a co-op at work? I'm sure they're distributing jam – but you probably aren't buying it! I'm sure the smart people all around you are instead!"

"Our co-op doesn't have jam."

"Well, then write a petition and have everybody sign it! Give it to your boss so he can do something about it! Today I was passing by the co-op of the hospital next door, and I saw the nurses, doctors and hospital administrators in line to buy jam! The whole universe is buying it and hoarding it, and we're just sitting here with our hands in our laps with not a worry in the world!"

"Will we die if we don't eat jam?"

"No, we won't die. If we don't eat meat, bread and cheese we won't die either. We'll live off the air. Whatever I tell you to buy and bring home, you always ask 'will we die if we don't eat it?' What if guests show up, like your brother with his wife and kids from Shiraz, what are you going to set on the table in front of them for breakfast? What are we going to have them eat their bread and butter with? Forget about us! We'll sleep hungry because of your thoughtlessness and die. But what about our guests? And it was always like this! If it weren't for me thinking of our life, we wouldn't even have these two old rugs and broken furniture and four dishes! Oh, how unlucky I was to end up with you!"

The woman's silhouette took over the whole curtain as she sobbed. Mr. Zeinali's voice could be heard, "Are you crying over jam?"

"No, I'm crying over my own misfortune. I don't know what I've done for God to put me here in this house with you and feel ashamed to ask you to buy and bring home two jars of jam like a thousand other people do! Then tomorrow when my dear old mom and pop leave their house to come here to see their daughter, and I don't even have any jam to serve them!"

"I am not a jam eater. If your mom and dad want jam, let them bring their own with them to eat here."

"Thankfully, I'm healthy and strong and can do it myself. If you won't do it, tomorrow morning I'll go after the jam myself. If I don't fill this shelf with jam tomorrow, you can call me whatever you like! I'll call my brother to come and square away my business with you! I'm sick and tired of living with you and your attitude!"

Jalal's mother said, "It's not right to eavesdrop on people's conversations. They might not want anybody to hear their talk.

Come away from the window. How bad these apartments are! If you even cough, everybody can hear you!"

"Mother, shall we go in the morning to file the complaint?"

"You're pushing it too far! Take care of your studies! You have a test the day after tomorrow!"

"If you're not coming, then I'll go on my own."

"If you go, then you'll see what happens! How dare you think you can just go on your own here and there to file a complaint! You have a mother!"

The silhouettes of Jalal and his mother could be seen in the window from the lower floor, as the sound of their argument filled the air. Mr. Zeinali said, "It's not right to listen in on people's arguments. Let's move away from the window. What bad apartments these are! A person can't even have an argument in them!"

Chapter Fourteen

Two representatives from the Shabdar Jam factory paid a visit to Ahmad, the corner grocer.

"Hello, sir."

"Hello there, how can I help you?"

"We're trying to find the address for that little boy who came into your store for the first time complaining that his jar of jam wouldn't open. We've been trying to find out where he lives for a few days but we haven't been able to."

"Well, I'm not sure of the exact address, but I think he lives on one of the streets right around here. You know, I don't know exactly where my customers live."

"What did the boy say to you?"

"Well, he was furious. He said he was going to file a complaint against the Shabdar factory and had even filled out the complaint form. He showed it to me. He also went to the Health Ministry. He is supposed to go back there with his mother. I told your distributors before to watch out and be careful. But you never told me why those jars wouldn't open. What's going on?"

"There was some technical problem. The technical supervisor is looking into it."

"Your jams weren't poisoned, were they? Some people say they caused cancer."

"What rubbish! Those are just rumors. Why do you believe that stuff! Where can we find this young man?"

"He usually passes by here on his way home from school. The kids all pass by here and he is usually with them. You'll see him on the sidewalk if you wait. Park your car a few streets down or you'll get a ticket. The kids will be out of school in a half an hour."

"We wouldn't be able to recognize him. You'll have to show him to us."

"If I see him, I certainly will."

One of the representatives went and sat in the car, and one waited on the sidewalk. When school was out, the children poured onto the sidewalks with their backpacks and books in hand. The representatives were scanning the faces of the children to see which one might be Jalal. The kids chatted with one another as they walked by, just like little birds chirping in the trees, hopping all over the place like you've never seen. The representative was listening in on the chatter, trying to discern who was talking about jam, but as was the rule of the day, they were all talking about jam! It made him dizzy turning his head every time he heard the word "jam"! He went inside to get the grocer's help.

"Come out show us which one of them is the little boy."

The kids crowded in with the customers in the shop:

"Sir, give me two colas please!"

"Sir, I want an ice cream cone!"

"Ahmad sir, do you have any pencils? Not this one. Give me one with an eraser tip!"

"Ahmad, sir. I've been waiting here for an hour. Don't you want to help me?"

"What do you need, ma'am?"

"Don't you have any jam? Whatever kind you have, it doesn't matter. This child is killing me. He says everybody is buying jam and he wants to buy some too! I tell him I'll make him some at home. But he refuses and says he wants the kind that comes in a jar. Please give me a jar. Don't you have any?"

"No ma'am. Where would I get it? The factories have recalled all their jams. Whatever I had, sold out in a half an hour. For the past ten days I've had to turn away all my jam customers."

"Sir, are you buying empty, lidded jam jars?"

"No ma'am! What use would they be to me? The jars must be full of jam!"

"Sir, do you have any dates?"

The kids were climbing all over each other in the chaos. The representative asked, "Aren't you going to come out and show the boy to us? They're all leaving."

"Stop bothering me. Can't you see I'm busy?"

Jalal and his friends walked right past the factory representative who was sitting in his car - and the man didn't know it was him.

Chapter Fifteen

Mrs. Zeinali was on her way home from grocery shopping carrying a bag of vegetables and yogurt. The two men were standing by a car at the entrance to her alleyway. They looked perplexed and in distress as they looked around aimlessly and approached passersby to ask questions.

Mrs. Zeinali went up to them, "Are you looking for someone, sir?"

"Yes, but we can't find him. They told us he lives on one of these streets. We've been looking all over the neighborhood for him for several days now."

"Who is it you're looking for? What does he do?"

"He's a boy who bought some jam from the corner grocer a few days ago, and is filing a complaint because the lid won't..."

"Oh yes! I know who he is! That's Jalal, our neighbor. Are you here from the factory?"

"Yes, that's right."

"He came over to our house a few nights ago to ask my husband to help him with the complaint against your company. His mother doesn't agree with going forward with the complaint. She says it's no use. But the boy isn't giving up."

"So you know him."

"Yes, sir. He lives upstairs from us. Their financial situation isn't very good, poor things. A few years ago, his father was hit by a car and God rest his soul, he died instantly. Sorry if I walk ahead of you."

"No problem, just please show us where he lives."

Mrs. Zeinali led them down the street. One of the factory representatives carried her groceries for her. "Excuse me for asking, sir, but where can a person find good quality but low cost jams these days?"

"How much do you want to buy?"

"About 20-30 jars. Of course, it should be good quality, and the lids should open! I want them for myself, but I also want to take a few jars to the boarding school. I volunteer there."

"Ma'am, how well do you know your neighbor Jalal and his mother? What kind of folk are they?"

"They are good – very nice people. His mother is decent and hard-working, and Jalal isn't a bad boy. You didn't hear this from me, but that mother and son are always arguing. We hear them or see their shadows through the curtains fighting all the time. That boy is demanding and stubborn. Of course, don't imagine that we want to interfere in their affairs, but we're neighbors, and we can't plug our ears all the time. It's an apartment house. Well we're here now. They live upstairs. But they aren't home right now."

"Ma'am I have one more question for you. That mother and son aren't too firm, are they?"

"What do you mean?"

"I mean, do you think they'll come to an agreement with us?"

"Well, I don't know about that. I just know that that boy is determined to file his complaint."

Chapter Sixteen

Ring went the doorbell. "Who is it? Jalal! Go see who is at the door!"

Before he opened the door, he went to the window to look out and see who was there. There were two men by the outside door, one was bald and holding a bouquet of flowers, and the other one held a box of pastries and something else in a plastic bag.

Mrs. Zeinali also peeked out the window. She ran upstairs. "They're here from the jam factory. They came here this morning, but you weren't home."

Jalal said, "They're just here to win us over. Don't open the door. Ahmad the grocer told me they've been looking all over for me."

Mrs. Zeinali said, "I told them you live here."

Ring! Mother said, "They're ringing again. It's not right for them to be left there by the door."

They were both happy. Mother and son looked at each other and smiled. Jalal puffed himself up with pride and his mother looked at him adoringly.

Mrs. Zeinali said, "Why are you looking at each other that way? One of you should go and open the door!"

Jalal said, "You go open it, mother."

"You stay here and a grown woman like me go and open the door?!"

Ring. Mrs. Zeinali went downstairs and opened the door. "Come in, please. They are at home now."

One of the men handed the carton of jam to Mrs. Zeinali. "Here is your jam. There are thirty jars of all varieties. Great quality!"

"Thank you very much! How much do I owe you?"

"It's no problem. Are Jalal and his mother upstairs?"

The carton of jam was heavy. Mrs. Zeinali called out to her husband, "Zeinali, come and get this carton of jam and carry it inside for me." Zeinali didn't hear, or at least he pretended not to. He didn't help and she was furious.

Chapter Seventeen

"Those good-for-nothings weren't able to get the jar of jam away from that kid."

"Why not? Didn't they find his house?"

"Yes, they did. They even took flowers and pastries. No matter what they did, they weren't able to get the jar from the kid. The mother and son said they didn't have the jar anymore. That's why we think they just want something more. They even promised the kid a football for the jar of jam and for giving up his claim. But they didn't accept the offer. We've got to think of another way."

As they spoke, the head of the factory picked up and examined the new jar designed and ordered by the technical supervisor. It was a beautiful hourglass designed jar with a nice-looking motif on it of a large pair of cherries on the stem with leaves. "It looks great, don't you think?"

"Yes, and it's a smaller jar than the last one, which saves us 30% in jam content. But the main thing is that this jar is beautiful. And the lid will be made out of plastic so as not to have the problems of a metal lid, and open easily."

"Did we ever find out the problem with that last lid and why the jars wouldn't open?"

"I'm still investigating that."

"How long is your investigation supposed to take?"

Chapter Eighteen

Every night in the middle of the night you could hear the yelling and screaming coming from Mr. Zeinali's house. Jalal and his mother would appear at the window and see the claws-and-teeth silhouette through their neighbor's curtains. You could hear Mrs. Zeinali's voice.

"Well, just go to sleep! Leave those poor old people alone!"

"I can't, I can't, madam! They're driving me crazy! One minute they're turning on the faucet. Another minute they're opening and shutting the refrigerator. Or it's the bathroom door. Just now one of them went into the kitchen and dropped a big pot on the floor! BANG! They won't let me sleep!"

"They're only visiting us for a short while. You just can't stand to see them eat at your table. Just grin and bear it. They'll be gone in a few days."

"They are welcome here. Let them stay. Let them stay a whole year if they want to. But don't let them eat so much jam. How much jam are you feeding them anyway? You're killing these poor people with the jam!"

"I'm not feeding it to them! They're eating it themselves! I'm afraid if the jam isn't eaten it will go bad and start to mold and maybe give someone food poisoning. So they're really doing us a favor."

"Well, when they eat so much jam, it makes them thirsty and then they have to drink water. And when they drink so much water, they have to go to the bathroom a lot. And the hinges in the bathroom door are loud and squeaky. "

"Instead of complaining so much, why don't you oil the door hinges tomorrow?"

"No, madam! It's not about thirst. I think their blood sugar has gone up and they're getting diabetes. Take them to get a blood test to find out why they are so restless at night. After all, you're their daughter. Why don't you take better care of them? Why did you buy all this jam in the first place for them to eat it and get diabetes?"

"I didn't buy it all for us to eat. I bought a carton for the boarding school."

"I hope those poor kids don't get sick."

"They're kids! They won't get sick!"

"Why not? Too much of anything is not good for you."

The screeching sound of the squeaky door and the sound Mrs. Zeinali's father gulping water broke the night silence in the house and made Mr. Zeinali wince. "How much jam is left?"

"About ten to twelve jars."

The old man couldn't see very well. He kept knocking things off the countertop in the kitchen. BANG!

Chapter Nineteen

Before the movie started, the sound of an announcer with a rich voice filled the air:

What do you eat with your bread and butter?

Then it shows a plump, little boy with fresh face puckering his lips as he says:

Shabdar jam!

Then it shows an hourglass shaped jar with a beautiful motif of cherries on the stem with leaves as the announcer says:

What is your favorite jam?

A darling, little girl with jam all over her lips says demurely:

All kinds, strawberry, sour cherry, cherry, fig and marmalade.

Then it shows all the children spinning and twirling as the announcer says in a deep voice:

Yes, all varieties of jam by Shabdar.

Jalal watched the program and went to bed.

The next morning, the sunlight shone through the window onto a jar of jam on top of the refrigerator. The jar glistened in the sunlight.

Chapter Twenty

There were white horses in the alley, stamping their feet and whinnying. The neighbors were all hanging their heads out their windows watching the horses outside.

There were two riders wearing strange clothes, like the clothes soldiers wore in olden times with red, cone-shaped hats with a fringe tassel hanging from the tip, rose-colored overcoats with gleaming buttons, fringed epaulets and tall, blue boots. The riders were holding the reins of the horses as they waited.

Mother was eating bread and jam as fast as she could. The riders shouted, "Hurry and come down!"

Jalal said to his mother, "Hurry, you're going to be late!"

Mother replied, "Let me eat something first. I'm so hungry!" and as she ate, she yelled, "You're making me nervous! See what you've done? Now I've spilled jam on my dress!"

Mother was wearing her most beautiful dress, the one she had worn to Mr. Hajizadeh's daughter, Shahla's wedding. The jam had spilled onto mother's dress and the stain wouldn't come out.

Jalal was anxious. "Hurry up, mother!"

The riders on horseback were blocking the alleyway. Mr. Ahmad, the corner grocer was trying to pass through with his cart. On the cart was a big barrel of jam and a ladle with which he was spooning out jam for the neighbors. Ladies would come out of their houses with their bowls in hand, Mr. Ahmad would spoon out a ladle full of jam into their bowls and take their money.

A woman was wearing a white smock. It was that same lady wearing the white smock that he had seen at the Health Ministry where he had gone to file his complaint. She was yelling and screaming. People were gathering all around. Mr. Ahmad pushed his cart forward to where he was blocked from going any further by the horses.

With the jam stain on her dress, mother went down the stairwell of the building. Jalal grabbed his jar of jam with the lid that wouldn't open and ran after his mother. Mr. Ahmad hit the horse's leg with his cart, and the riders yelled at him, "These horses are government property!"

Jalal and his mother got onto the horses as the riders took the reins and went out of the alleyway. Women and men watched from their windows. Jalal held his head high and looked back at his neighbors with pride. The horses passed the streets. Lines of people watched the horses and riders, Jalal and his mother in the streets as they went.

There was a large banquet hall. Furniture lined the room with women and men sitting all around. When Jalal and his mother got off the horses, two men came to escort them into the banquet hall. There was an orchestra playing music. Jalal and his mother walked past all the people.

One man was sitting up at the head of the room dressed in white from head to toe. On his chest was a flag. He motioned for Jalal and his mother to sit at the front. They walked forward and the man said, "Give me the jar."

Jalal gave him the jar. All the men and women cheered, and the man opened the jar in one twist. The orchestra played a happy song as he handed Jalal a golden statue and said, "Bravo young man. I'm pleased that there are young people like you in our country with so much diligence and attention, and who don't take anything for granted and who are able to..."

"It's time to get up, Jalal! You sleep too much and were talking in your sleep! What were you saying? Come on, get up. You'll be late for school!"

Jalal rubbed his eyes, looked around and smiled. He looked at the jar of jam on top of the refrigerator, the one with the lid that wouldn't open.

Chapter Twenty-one

Adhesive bandages had gone up in price and were hard find anywhere. The pharmacies were selling two individual adhesive bandages with the purchase of medicines. Cuts on hands and arms and legs and feet were increasing by the day.

There was such a surplus of jam in homes that the likelihood of people and their kids dropping jars and breaking them was much more prevalent than ever before. They would cut their hands when picking up the broken glass or injure their feet by stepping on a stray piece of broken glass. Those who had purchased jam along with adhesive bandages during the co-op sales were happy.

Spilt jam everywhere was attracting flies. Cockroaches and ants were filling the holes and crevices in the doors and closets. There were a jillion ants under the carpets, in between the sofa cushions and in the bed sheets. Ants would find their way into people's noses and ears at night, and wake them from their sound sleep, put them in a bad mood. Suffering from a lack of sleep, people would grumble and gripe and argue with each other. For this reason, cotton swabs became very useful.

Jam was getting all over everything and making everything sticky: the rugs, the car seats, the kitchen floor. The ants loved it! They were proliferating more and more each day. Ants would climb up pant legs and sleeves, tickle people and make them uncomfortable. Sometimes an ant would climb up the pant leg of a car driver and annoy him, cause him to hit the car in front of him, and force him to resort to begging the other driver for mercy.

Everyone was trying to get their hands on bug spray, but the price kept going up despite the weather getting colder and colder. You couldn't find rug shampoo anywhere.

Mrs. Zeinali had taken her elderly parents to get a blood test, suspecting their blood sugar at skyrocketing levels. Many people's blood sugar had gone up, which is why the waiting room was so crowded. Mrs. Zeinali was waiting with her parents for their turn to receive the lab results. An angry man was sitting across from them on a bench, yelling, "They should recall these jams! Take the jam away from people. People are ruining their kidneys and hearts, and going blind! People shouldn't eat so much jam! Throw it away! It's better to lose your investment than to lose your health, go blind or have a heart attack, or moan from pain in your kidneys and chest all night! Is that what you want, people?"

A plump lady sitting next to him said, "Would you really throw it all away? What kind of person would throw away jam that so much work went into and for which she waited so long in line to buy with coupons from the co-op coupon booklet? I'll eat it so that our children and grandchildren won't eat it. I've lived my life."

133

"Then eat it and get fat! And go take a blood test to see how high your blood sugar goes up! And if you get sick, don't complain to me about it! And don't moan all night and get up twenty times a night to drink water and use the bathroom!" The woman got up and walked away, refusing to talk to him anymore.

The lab results came back for Mrs. Zeinali's parents. Her mother's blood sugar was high, and it was affecting her eyesight. Her father's was even higher, and it made everything blurry in his vision. Father said, "What do I do now?" Mother said, "This is what happens when you can't control yourself and eat too much jam!"

Mrs. Zeinali said, "Father dear, don't worry. Take your medicines and keep away from jam. Take daily walks and your blood sugar will gradually come down." Father said, "Let's go to the boarding school to see the kids. I'm a teacher. I've spent my whole life with kids. I want to see them. I want to see them every day for as long as my eyes can see. Take me to the park. I want to see the trees and flowers and birds. I want to see my grandchildren, before my whole life goes dark." He had a lump of sadness in his throat as he got up from his chair.

They left the laboratory. They came to a man who had stacked up the old jam jars on the sidewalk and was yelling, "Jam! Jam! Half-price Jam! All kinds – all varieties!"

Mrs. Zeinali stopped and looked at the jam. She turned to her mother, "How inexpensive! It's a real deal!" She picked out four jars of jam: fig, peach, rose petal and carrot. "We'll use these eventually. And very shortly we'll have to pay four times the price for these same jams!"

They kept walking. At the corner a little further down the street was an old man sitting outside the pharmacy selling canes. Mrs. Zeinali's father stopped and picked out a handsome cane with a comfortable handle. He took it in hand and continued walking.

As they walked down the sidewalk they could see all kinds of buttons all over the ground: white, black, brown, pink, small, large, from men's shirts and women's overcoats, from people who had gotten fat and burst their buttons. Mrs. Zeinali's mother was bending over and picking them up as she went.

Chapter Twenty-two

One morning, a brand new, midnight blue car pulled up in front of Jalal's house. Jalal had been waiting in front of the window for days to see a car from the Shabdar Jam Factory come after him. When he saw this, it made him very happy. He looked again, and saw a young, well-dressed man get out of the car and walk up to his house. He rang the second floor doorbell.

"Mother, mother, they're here! They've come themselves! They've finally come from the jam factory!"

"I knew they would show up!"

Mother and Jalal sat in the back seat of that new, midnight blue car. Jalal was wearing his brand new shirt and socks. He was happy and felt victorious as he went to the factory. He was holding his jar of jam as he walked ahead of them past the people, boxes, machines and big vats of jam. The laborers were lined up on either side clapping for him and greeting him. Mother and the young man were walking one step behind Jalal, and by the greetings the people were expressing to the young man, you could tell he was somebody important.

When they arrived at the front of the factory office building, the young man turned to Jalal and his mother and said, "Come on in, you are welcome here. I am the owner's son and this is my father's office."

He gestured towards a large office full of furniture and chairs, and then left to take care of his business.

The factory owner was a small man who didn't look like the head of a factory. He had fired the general manager and was now handling everything himself. He gestured for Jalal and his mother to sit down on the chairs in front of his desk. He coughed and said, "I thank you both for bringing this matter to our attention. If you had not pursued this matter so diligently, it might have been months or even years before we discovered our mistake. It's not just about the factory closing or a hefty fine. What's important is that no consumer ever pursued the issue of why the jars wouldn't open. They would all run boiling water over the lid, whereas the issue was much more important than that. After you've had your tea, we'll go together and I'll show you what the problem was, so that you'll rest assured that we haven't been sitting on our hands all this time, and that we have discovered what the problem was."

Mother and Jalal drank their tea and got up. Jalal grabbed a cookie and popped it into his mouth. Mother looked at him sternly as if to say, "Mind your manners!"

The factory head took Jalal's jar from him, the one that wouldn't open, and the three of them together left the room. They walked down a hallway to a room where above the door was a brass plate which was inscribed in a calligraphic style, "Technical Engineering".

When they entered the room, they saw a technical engineer wearing a long white smock that appeared to be too tight for his increasing girth. He was overall a jolly-looking man. On the table off to the side were various jars full of jam and a microscope. When the engineer saw Jalal and his mother standing there, he said, "It was right about noon when I was eating lunch and wondering why these jars wouldn't open. All of a sudden, my eyes fell upon the bottle of cola on my table, which I had half-way finished with my rice and stew. Yes, I noticed that the bottle was crooked. At first, I thought that something was underneath the bottle, making it look crooked. So I cleared the table of anything that might be underneath it, and set it squarely on the table. But it still looked crooked. I held the bottle in the palm of my hand and closed my left eye to examine it carefully. Yes, it was crooked for sure. Then I took one of the jars of jam that wouldn't open and placed it in the palm of my hand, and then placed it on the table in the cleared spot, and looked at it from a distance. I closed my left eye and saw that the jar was indeed crooked. The laborer at the jar factory had apparently set the glass mould crookedly, by about 2 millimeters, before securing it. He didn't even notice that for about a week or ten days, the factory was producing crooked jars. During the stage of securing the lids to the jars, there was no difficulty, because the closing of the lids on the jars was done by factory machines. But when consumers tried to open the jars, all they got was grief because the lid wasn't secure to the mouth of the jar, and the threads around the rim were uneven. No matter what the consumer did to open the jar was to no avail."

The factory owner added, "And no amount of boiling water would help."
Jalal added, "And wedging the tip of a knife under the lid wouldn't help either."
Mother added, "The consumer would moan and groan and curse!"
The factory owner said, "The consumer cursed us whereas he should have tried to find the reason for the problem, which is what you did! Bravo!"
The engineer, "Let's go. The head of the jar making factory is waiting for us. I spoke

141

with him earlier, and I told him he had the responsibility to answer to this young man and his mother." The engineer took the Jalal's jar of jam in hand, and led them out of his office.

Jalal and his mother got into the car and they all went to the jar-making factory. They passed by the laborers and the machines. The engineer was walking ahead of them, carrying that jar. Jalal and his mother followed behind. The jam factory owner didn't join them, as he probably had some other business to attend to.

The laborers at the jar factory looked at the jar, and at Jalal and his mother as they greeted them. The head of the jar-making factory came out to greet them, and took delivery of the defective jar from the engineer and led them in another direction. The engineer went back to the jam factory.

The head of the jar-making factory kept talking to Jalal and his mother as he walked ahead of them. "The area of our factory is 3877.50 square meters of land, with 1423 square meters of construction. It was founded in 1977 and has 214 laborers and employees made up of 40 women and the rest, men. We have founded a co-op for our employees and hope to provide housing for them as well. We also furnish our employees with uniforms and safety helmets and shoes but unfortunately some of them are still careless and inattentive. The example is this one here." And they reached an employee who was busy measuring a soda bottle. When he noticed the boss standing there with Jalal and his mother, he stopped what he was doing and stood straight up and said, "Hello."

The boss handed Jalal's jar to him and said, "Open the lid of this jar, Mr. Ghaffouri."

He took the jar and struggled with it. Then he squinted at it, examining it carefully with one eye and said, "Yes, if you could please excuse me from my post for one hour, I would like to take this young man and his mother somewhere and come right back. Would it be ok if I used the company car?"

The employee got into the front passenger's seat while Jalal and his mother sat in the back. He said to the driver, "Let's go" and turned to Jalal and his mother and said, "Forgive me that my back is to you."

The company car wound its way through the city until they reached the front of Jalal's school. Jalal and his mother's eyes were wide open with surprise. "What is the meaning of this?!" they said as they got out of the car and walked into the school.

The employee was carrying the jar as they walked past the children in the school yard. Jalal and his mother were following him, looking at each other quizzingly and didn't know why he had brought them there.

The children were all teasing them as Jalal walked through the school yard with his mother and the factory employee. The assistant supervisor came forward, "How can I help you?"

The factory employee said, "I'm Hossein Ghaffouri's father. I'd like to speak with him."

The assistant supervisor turned to Jalal and his mother and said, "How can I help you? You already called this morning to inform us that Jalal wouldn't be here today."

The factory employee said, "They are here with me. I want to introduce my son to this lady and her son."

Jalal already knew the boy. They were classmates and the boy sat right behind Jalal in the classroom. He had a long, slender neck, always wore a plaid shirt, and wasn't a very bright student.

The assistant supervisor was confused and couldn't figure out what the jar of jam, Jalal, his mother and Ghaffouri's father all had to do with one another.

He said to Jalal, "What's this jar of jam doing back here at the school?"

The factory employee said, "I brought it. Where is my son?"

"Just wait a while." The assistant supervisor monitored his watch carefully and then sounded the recess bell. The children spilled into the school yard. The assistant supervisor paged Ghaffouri. The father and son were standing next to each other in the school yard.

The father held up the jar of jam and yelled at him, "This crooked jar with a lid that won't open is the result of that day when the school suspended you because your hair was not properly cut. When your mother called the factory and told me they had thrown you out of school, it was just like taking a blow to the head! I was so angry with you that I set the jar mould lopsidedly!"

His yelling rang throughout the schoolyard. The kids all gathered around the father holding the jar of jam up high so everybody could see. Several boys were off to the side of the school yard playing soccer. One of the boys punted the ball, and it went flying through the air and hit the jar Mr. Ghaffouri was holding up. The jar went crashing down and broke into pieces. Jam was all over the ground. But the lid was still on the broken jar.

Jalal looked bitterly at his broken jar of jam. He bit his lip and left. The assistant supervisor said, "Recess is over! Kids get back to class."

Chapter Twenty-three

Two of the boarding school girls were acting as mischievous as two little birds chirping and giggling with laughter. Mrs. Zeinali's parents were standing off to the side of the yard. Mr. Zeinali was holding a plastic bag full of his medicines, leaning on his cane, smiling as he watched the children playing in the yard.

The children were wearing the new uniforms that had been provided for them. Mrs. Zeinali was still helping the little ones put them on.

She noticed that the buttonholes had not been sewn in correctly, and so when the buttons were fastened, it caused unsightly ripples in the fabric between the buttons.

The children looked unhappily and with surprise at the ripples, which they tried to smooth out with their hands. But the ripples would come right back.

But they were so happy to have the new clothes that they were able to overlook a few wrinkles. One little girl raised her index finger in permission to ask a question and said, "Madam, why are there ripples in the front of all our uniforms? Why aren't they smooth?"

About the Author

Houshang Moradi-Kermani was born in 1944 in Sirch Village near the city of Kerman in south central Iran. After completing elementary school in his village and middle school in Kerman, he studied dramatic arts in Tehran where he subsequently attended university, finally earning a B.A. in English translation. He began his career in the arts on the radio in Kerman and Tehran in 1961.

Numerous works by Houshang Moradi Kermani have been published including The Stories of Majid, Children of the Carpet Weaving House, The Palm, The Water Urn, Fist on Hide, The Tandoor and Other Stories, Anar's Smile, Mommy's Guest, The Cruse, Sweet Jam, Like the Full Moon, Nine of Each Kind, You're No Stranger Here, Rice and Stew, and The Water Storage. His works have been translated into English, French, German, Spanish, Dutch, Arabic, Armenian, Chinese, Korean, Greek and Turkish. His books have resulted in thirty eight television serial episodes and feature films for cinema, and have been entered in domestic and foreign film festivals.

Houshang Moradi Kermani has won many awards for his works such as the Book of the Year, awarded by the Ershad

Ministry of Culture, as well as many other awards from various bodies such as the Institute for the Intellectual Development of Children and Young Adults, the Children's Book Council, the Fajr Film Festival, the Esfahan Children's and Young Adult's Film Festival, the Association for the Protection of Children's Rights, and the Headquarters of the Respected Supreme Leader.

Translations of his works have won numerous awards from many foreign cultural and art institutes such as, the International Board on Books for Young People (IBBY), the Jury for the Hans Christian Anderson (1992 Berlin – Distinguished Author), C.P.N.B. (Collective Promotion for the Dutch Book), the Institute for German Youth, the Austrian Ministry of Culture and Art, Switzerland's Blue Cobra Book Award, the "Jose Martini" literary award of Costa Rica, the Munich and Sweden International Libraries, Unicef and was nominated for the Astrid Lindgren Memorial Award (**ALMA**).

He is a member of the Kerman Studies Foundation and a standing member of the Persian Language and Literature Academy. He is a university professor.

In 2005, he won recognition as one of Iran's lasting and influential literary figures in the field of literature for children and young adults.

About the Translator

Caroline Croskery has spent her life within the Persian culture. She was born in the United States and moved to Iran at the age of twenty-one. She holds a Bachelor's Degree from the University of California at Los Angeles in Iranian Studies where she graduated Cum Laude. For many years, she has been active in three fields of specialization: Language Teaching, Translation and Interpretation and Voiceover Acting.

During her thirteen years living in Iran, she taught English and also translated as well as dubbed Iranian feature films into English. After returning to live in the United States, she began a ten year career as a court interpreter and translator of books from Persian into English. She is an accomplished voiceover talent, and currently continues her voiceover career in both English and Persian.

Other titles translated and narrated by Caroline Croskery are:

Languor of the Morn, by Fattaneh Haj Seyed Javadi

We Are All Sunflowers, by Erfan Nazarahari

Democracy or Democrazy, by Seyed Mehdi Shojaee

The Water Urn, by Houshang Moradi Kermani

In the Twinkling of an Eye, by Seyed Mehdi Shojaee

A Vital Killing: A Collection of Stort Stories from the Iran-Iraq War by Ahmad Dehghan

The Little Goldfish, with Audio CD Narration by Katayoun Riahi

Mullah Nasreddin, illustrated by Alireza Golduzian

The Paper Boat, written and illustrated by Anahita Taymourian

The Circus Outside the Window, written and illustrated by Anahita Taymourian

Sleep Full of Sheep, written and illustrated by Pejman Rahimizadeh

Stillness in a Storm, Collection of Poetry in Persian and English with Audio CD by Saeid Ramezani

47288153R00096

Made in the USA
Charleston, SC
07 October 2015